by
Judy Sierra

pictures by
Marc Brown

Alfred A. Knopf New York

One blustery morning, when frosty winds blew,
When families stayed home, and when field trips were few,
The midwinter doldrums arrived at the zoo.

Little lemurs stopped leaping.
Their yowling was keeping
The wombats awake.
Then the snakes (by mistake)
Tied themselves up in knots.
Ocelots lost their spots.

Owls did not give a hoot.

Pandas quit being cute.

Even penguins were surly.

The zoo gates closed early.

Then, just when it seemed that the doldrums had won—
That the zoo never, ever again would be fun—
A very large hippo collapsed in dismay
And a very *small* hippo hopped out of the way.
A young kangaroo shouted, "Look! Me hop, too!"
And together they hip-hopped all over the zoo.

It was simply amazing what two friends could do
When they tapped, and they rapped, and they twirled on their feet.
All the animals rocked to the hip-aroo beat,
And slowly, the doldrums began to retreat.

"Woo-hoo!" cried the young kangaroo. "We're so-o-o musical!"

"Cool," said the hippo. "Let's put on a ZooZical."

Every creature had talent, there wasn't much to it.
They just needed the hippo to say, "We can do it!
We're born to be singers and dancers and acrobats."
ZooZical fever swept all the zoo's habitats.

The animals sang songs that everyone knew
(If the words weren't quite right, then they added a few),
And even giraffes, who were quiet and shy,
Discovered their voices could reach to the sky.

Oh my darling,
Oh my darling,
Oh my darling porcupine.
It's a tall world after all....
For he's a jolly gorilla....

And after they'd all learned the musical score,
They made posters and costumes and scenery galore.

Amazing
come to the
ZooZical

The news spread like wildfire. The zoo was aglow.
And in spite of the wind, and the sleet, and the snow,
The who's who of Springfield all rushed to the show.

At a quarter past eight, when the lemurs were certain
The moment was right, they flung open the curtain.
Onstage, the wee hippo blinked up at the light.
But her feet wouldn't move. She was frozen with fright.
Oh, no! Would the ZooZical turn out all right?

Yes!

A tiger backstage roared an ear-splitting roar,
And the hippo hopped higher than ever before.
She hit the ground tapping. The crowd started clapping.
(The young kangaroo didn't clap—he was napping.)

Bears walked the tightrope with elegant ease,
Flamingos whizzed by on the flying trapeze,
Raccoons danced in pairs, baboons danced in troops,
And snakes joined the dancers as live hula hoops.

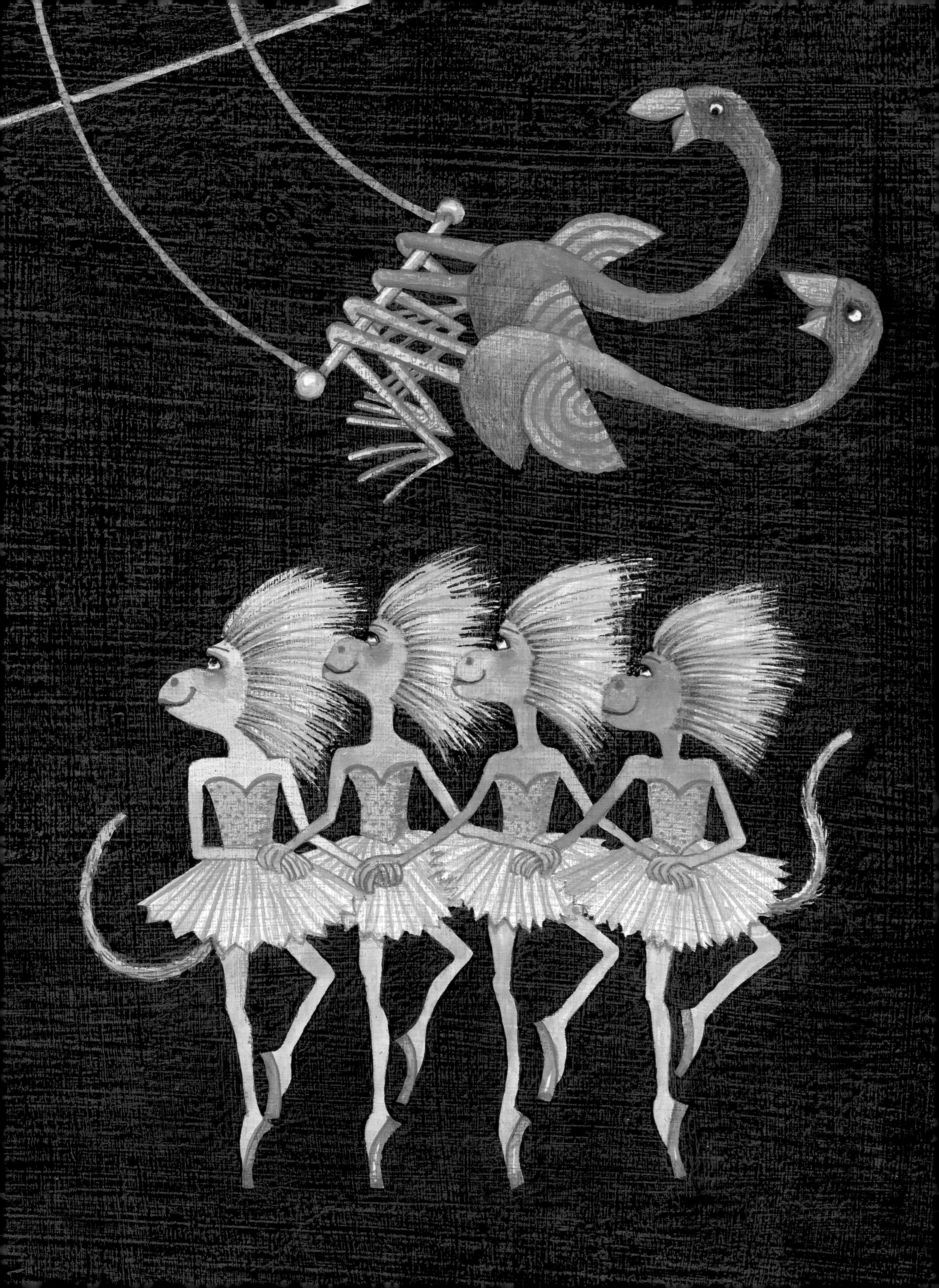

The crocodile kids led the "Alphabet Song,"
With the audience gleefully chanting along.

E
F
G
L
M
N
O
P
U
V
W
X
Y
Z

Then onto the stage rolled ten seals on a bus,
Barking, "Let's sing a tune that is all about us!"
ZOO BUS
The seals on the bus

go round and round. . .

And that young kangaroo? When he finally awoke, he
Delighted the crowd with a wild karaoke,
And everyone danced to the Zoo Hokey Pokey.

You put your right paw in,
You put your left hoof out....
That's what it's all about!

It was one of those times that you hope never ends,
When penguins and pandas and pythons are friends,
When tigers don't bite, when the doldrums take flight,
On a magical, musical ZooZical night.

For Alden and Maxine
—J.S.

For Isabella Brown, my favorite ZooZical
—M.B.

THIS IS A BORZOI BOOK PUBLISHED BY ALFRED A. KNOPF

Visit us on the Web! www.randomhouse.com/kids
Educators and librarians, for a variety of teaching tools, visit us at www.randomhouse.com/teachers
Library of Congress Cataloging-in-Publication Data
Sierra, Judy.
ZooZical / story by Judy Sierra ; pictures by Marc Brown. — 1st ed.
p. cm.
Summary: When the winter doldrums arrive at the zoo, a very small hippo and a young kangaroo decide to stage a "ZooZical," a show to display their singing, dancing, acrobatic, and other talents to the people of Springfield.
ISBN 978-0-375-86847-4 (trade) — ISBN 978-0-375-96847-1 (lib. bdg.)
[1. Stories in rhyme. 2. Talent shows—Fiction. 3. Zoo animals—Fiction. 4. Animals—Fiction.]
I. Brown, Marc Tolon, ill. II. Title.
PZ8.3.S577Zoo 2011
[E]—dc22
2010038565
The illustrations in this book were created using gouache on gessoed wood.
MANUFACTURED IN CHINA
August 2011
10 9 8 7 6 5 4 3 2 1
First Edition
Random House Children's Books supports the
First Amendment and celebrates the right to read.